Leo's Toy Store

By Warren Peace

Leo's Toy Store. -1st ed.
2013935132
ISBN-13: 978-0692584262
ISBN-10: 0692584269
Printed in the United States of America.

17-1563

For Jacob and Tyler

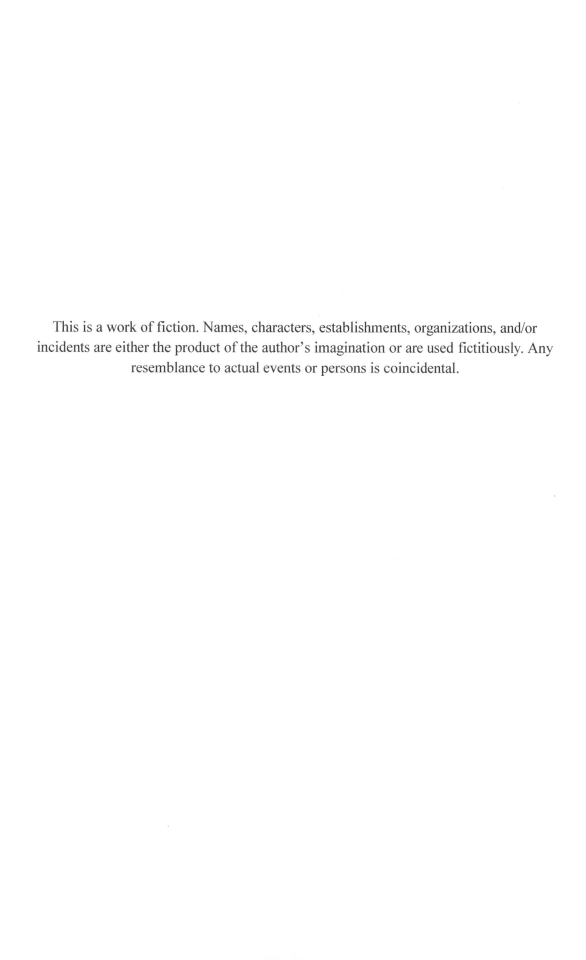

Leo's Toy Store

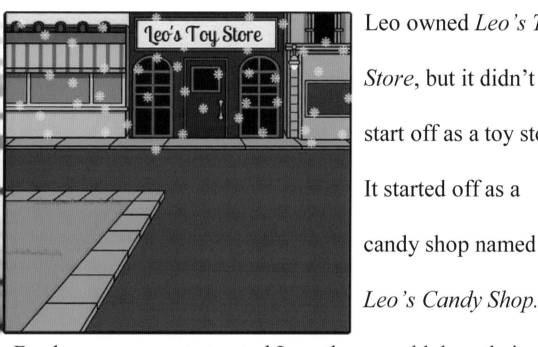

Leo owned *Leo's Toy Store*, but it didn't start off as a toy store. It started off as a candy shop named *Leo's Candy Shop.*

But because parents trusted Leo, they would drop their children off for Leo to watch while they ran errands. The children would get bored with nothing to do and so Leo started bringing toys to the store for the children to play with. Eventually he realized he could earn more and that the children would have more fun if he sold toys in his store in addition to candy.

Before long the toys sold more than his candy, so Leo changed the name of his store to *Leo's Toy Store*.

Though he didn't sell as much candy as he used to, he still enjoyed having it for his customers and, because of his generous heart, he would often give away peppermints, liquorice, peanut brittle, chocolates, and other sweet treats to the children who visited his store.

Leo had owned and managed his store since he was a young man.

He and his dog, Tug, were loved by the people of their town and many of the townsfolk would stop by to give Tug a dog biscuit or other treat.

Unlike other toy stores, Leo allowed children to play with the toys even if they didn't buy them. It warmed his heart that the children got such enjoyment from playing together with the toys in his shop.

Every year Leo looked forward to Christmas. Not just because of the increase in business for his shop, but because he got to see so many happy faces as children and parents came to his store.

This year Leo also looked forward to meeting the new owner of the building he rented.

Leo had known the previous owner the entire time he had owned his store but that man had left his business to his son, James.

James had taken over the business last week and was scheduled to meet with Leo today.

James was just about to leave to go to meet Leo when his phone rang.

"Hello?"

"Hi, Daddy!" his son Joshua exclaimed. "We haven't gone to watch the trains during lunch in a long time. Can we go today?"

James looked at his watch.

"Not today, son, I've got appointments to keep. Maybe some time soon."

"But, Daddy, it's been so long since we've watched trains or even played with our trains."

"I know, son, I miss it too, but I'm just too busy. I've got to earn more money. You understand, right, son?"

"Umm...sure, Daddy."

"Alright, son, you get back to helping your mom decorate the Christmas tree. I'm probably going to be home late again tonight so you two should go ahead and eat without me. Bye, son, be a good boy."

"Bye, Dad."

James walked down the street toward *Leo's Toy Store.*
He walked in and looked at the candy and said to himself, "I
thought this was a toy store."

"Welcome!" Leo called from the back of the store as he
walked to the front counter. "How can I help you?"

"Mr. Leo, I'm James. I own this building."

"Nice to meet you, James! And please, call me Leo."

"Mr. Leo, I'm here
simply to inform you
that your rent will be
going up by twenty-
five percent, effective
immediately."

Leo's face fell. "I don't think I can afford that. The store is
just getting by."

"Well if you can't, we'll just get someone in here who can. You have to pick up the pace, Leo."

Leo couldn't find any words to say. He simply hung his head. James rolled his eyes and left.

That evening Leo and Tug walked two blocks in the snow to Leo's house.

Usually the snow brought a smile to Leo's face, but tonight he was troubled. As he held the door open for Tug, he let out a long sigh.

Leo dried the snow from his beard and sat in his favorite chair as he thought about what Mr. James had said.

"I don't know what we're going to do, Tug. I don't make enough money from the store to pay that much more in rent. I wish Carol was here. Nothing has been the same since she died. Without the store and the kids, I don't know what I'd do." Leo glanced at a picture of Carol on the wall.

Tug jumped into Leo's lap and licked his face. "Oh, thanks, boy. Don't worry, we'll figure something out. I'm not going to let it change the way I run the store. If this is going to be my last month with the store, I'm going to make sure people see the same Leo as always."

Leo ate his supper, read some of his book, and got ready for bed. During his prayers, he asked for the store to be saved.

The walk to the toy store the next morning seemed longer than usual to Leo as he searched his mind for ideas to save the store. "I don't want to raise prices. They're already high enough."

Leo walked into the store. The smell of the peppermint brought back memories of when he only sold candy. "I need to stick with what I said, Tug. I'm not going to change. People enjoy my store for what it is and it's going to stay that way as long as I'm here."

Just then some children ran into the store. "Good morning, Leo," one of them hollered. The children quickly found their favorite toys and started playing with them on the floor.

Leo smiled contently at the sound of their laughter.

He had enjoyed helping the smiling parents choose toys for their children. The snow fell outside and the temperature dropped which to Leo made it seem more like Christmas.

"Thanks, Leo, you're the best!" One mother had said when he helped her find the last pink teddy bear in the store.

"I know Laura will enjoy it!" Leo called after her.

Leo watched the children have a snowball fight on the sidewalk in front of his store and it wasn't long before they came inside to warm up. Leo welcomed them with hot chocolate.

Afterwards, some of the children bought Christmas gifts for their brothers and sisters. Others bought ornaments for their parents.

It couldn't have been a better day so far for Leo, all things considered.

The bell on the door rang out while Leo was checking inventory in the back room. He walked to his cash register and saw James walking toward him.

"Merry Christmas, James," Leo said with a small smile.

"We will see how merry it is, Mr. Leo. How is business going today?" James looked around the store, noticing children playing with toys and making more noise than he would like.

"It's going well, I'd say. Like most stores, we always have a jump in business before Christmas."

"Well maybe if you charged for this babysitting you'd be able to pay the new rent!"

"Well I...I," Leo stammered.

"Is this a daycare or a store, Mr. Leo?"

Before Leo could answer, James walked to the door and slammed it as he left. The children stopped playing and looked at Leo.

He saw their scared faces and responded with a calm smile. "It's alright, kids. Go ahead and play. I'm happy you're here during your Christmas break."

He handed candy canes to the children and gave them each a hug.

"Uncle Leo, why was that man so mad?" asked a little girl.

Other children gathered around to hear Leo's answer.

"Well, kids, maybe he's just so busy that he has no time to play. All work and no play can make people sad."

That evening Leo fed Tug supper but didn't feel like eating anything himself.

"It's best I accept it, Tug, we're going to lose the store. I just don't see any way around it."

Tug stood in front of Leo's chair and whimpered.

"I guess I'll start packing things up tomorrow. I hope I can send most of the toys back and get a refund. Three days until Christmas and it's not looking like it's going to be a good one this year."

Leo said his prayers and went to bed.

As he walked to the store the next morning, he reminded himself to be positive and cheerful.

"I'll be strong for the kids," he said to himself.

Leo opened the front door and turned the "closed" sign over to "open," then he went to the back room and gathered some empty boxes. The first toys he packed to ship were the ones that the children didn't play with in the store, like the board games. After filling several boxes with mostly board games, Leo sighed. "Tug, I need a cup of coffee."

The smell of brewing coffee filled the entire store. Even the children, who had already started to come into the store, said things like, "That smells good," and "I want a cup."

"How about some hot chocolate instead?" Leo asked as he started warming the milk. Most of the kids walked toward the back of the store following a toy car and Leo was so distracted by preparing the hot chocolate that he only heard the second time that a small voice called to him.

"Mr. Leo?"

He turned to see a small boy with a toy locomotive held out to him. "Yes, my friend?"

"How much is this?"

Leo turned the toy over and saw the price tag. "It's twenty dollars, son. Would you like me to wrap it?"

The boy lowered his head and spoke softly. "Oh, well I only have eight dollars. I wanted to buy a gift for my dad."

"What kinds of things does your dad enjoy?" Leo asked.

"He used to put together toy trains and tracks with me."

"But he doesn't anymore?" Leo asked.

"Well, he wanted to be a train conductor when he was a boy. But now he doesn't have time anymore."

The boy looked back at the train before returning his eyes to the floor.

Leo looked at the train in his hand and then back to the boy who held a tight fist around his eight dollars.

"How did you earn your eight dollars?"

"I raked my neighbor's leaves. Two times."

"Well I think that you earned this locomotive," Leo said as he reached out his hand.

The boy smiled. "Thank you so much, Mr. Leo!"

He gave Leo the eight dollars and Leo turned to wrap the toy. "Oh, no thank you. I don't want it wrapped."

Leo handed the toy to the boy who turned and ran out the door. Leo smiled and put the money in the cash register and then headed back to the boxes.

That evening the boy waited for his father to get home from work. He paced circles in the family's living room until he finally heard the front door open.

"Daddy!"

The boy put the locomotive behind his back and waited for his father to walk in the room.

"Daddy, I –"

"Joshua, I saw you at Leo's toy store today."

The boy nodded.

"Don't tell me you were wasting money on some – "

"No, Daddy, I wanted to get your Christmas present. I've been saving and I want to give it to you early."

The boy reached the locomotive out to his father, James.

"Since you don't have time anymore to go see the trains, I wanted to bring one to you."

Tears filled his eyes as James looked down at his son and the train in his hands. He dropped to his knees and hugged him.

Joshua told James how Leo had let him buy the train for only eight dollars when it was supposed to be twenty.

"He said he thought I'd earned it by raking the leaves."

The next morning was Christmas Eve. Usually it was a big day for *Leo's Toy Store*, but Leo had left the sign on the "closed" side today so that he could get some more packing finished. If he worked all day, he should be able to take Christmas Day off so that he could have lunch with his neighbor, Larry, whose sister came to visit as well.

Several children peered through the front windows at Leo. Occasionally he would stop and wave at them. They didn't understand what was going on and why Leo had the "closed" sign up and the door locked.

Finally Leo took a break and brought a dish of peanut brittle out to give to the children.

"Just one each now."

One little girl spoke up. "Why isn't the store open, Leo? It's Christmas Eve."

Leo smiled back. "It'll be alright, kids. But I'd rather not talk about it right now."

He walked back into the store and sat the empty dish next to the cash register. The bell to the front door jingled as someone entered. Leo had forgotten to lock it back. He turned to see James, in yet another nice suit.

"Don't worry, Mr. James, I should be finished packing today and the shipping people will be here the day after Christmas. Then I'll be out of the way."

"Actually, Leo, I wanted to talk to you. What you did for my son was very kind. And it taught me several lessons.

One is that there are things more valuable than money. Having someone rent this building who is loved by the town and who loves them is good for business. But it's also good because you helped me see that I should put people ahead of money, like you did."

James reached out to shake Leo's hand. "So, Leo, I won't be raising your rent."

A big hardy smile stretched across Leo's face. "Thank you so much, James! You've given me back something very special."

James looked at all the boxes near the back of the store. 'It looks like we have a lot of boxes to unpack."

Leo raised his eyebrows. "We?"

"I'm going to help you unpack, Leo. It's the least I can do."

So Leo got to keep *Leo's Toy Store.* And the children got to keep playing with toys even if they didn't buy them.

James still made appointments to come to *Leo's Toy Store*, but for a new reason.

He and Joshua would meet at least once a week during lunch to play with the toy trains in Leo's store.

And they were the first to know when Leo got a new shipment of different kinds of trains.

As for Tug, he continued to be a good friend to Leo and enjoyed the dog biscuits that visitors brought to the store for him.

He watched through the years as Leo brought joy to the lives of children and parents alike.

The End

Reflection and Memory Questions

1. Why did Leo change his candy shop into a toy store?

_____

_____

_____

2. Why did Leo still sell candy in Leo's Toy Store?

_____

_____

_____

3. What hobby did the owner of Leo's building, James, not have time for anymore?

_____

_____

_____

Why did James complain about Leo letting children play with toys in his store even if they didn't buy them?

_____

_____

_____

Why do you think Leo let Ben buy the toy locomotive for only eight dollars when the price was twenty dollars?

_____

_____

_____

_____

_____

_____

. **What lessons did James tell Leo that he had learned from his (Leo's) kindness to Ben?**

_____

_____

_____

_____

_____

_____

_____

. **What were some of Leo's good traits?**

_____

_____

_____

_____

8. What were some of James' good traits?

_____

_____

_____

_____

9. What was the name of Leo's dog? _____

10. Who was Leo's late wife? _____

For more books by James Laymond Publishing, visit http://www.JamesLaymond.com

For more books by Warren Peace, visit http://WarrenPeace.com

Made in the USA
Columbia, SC
04 December 2017